The Beginner's Bible

Wild About Creation

Sticker & Activity Book

ZONDERkidz

Copyright © 2015 by Zonderkidz

Published in Grand Rapids, Michigan, by Zonderkidz. Zonderkidz
is a registered trademark of The Zondervan Corporation, L.L.C.,
a wholly owned subsidiary of HarperCollins Christian Publishing, Inc.

Requests for information should be addressed to
customercare@harpercollins.com.

ISBN: 978-0-310-74705-5

Design: Diane Mielke

Printed in Slovenia

24 25 26 /GPS/ 12 11 10 9 8

Let There Be Light!

In the beginning, the world was empty. Darkness was everywhere. But God had a plan! God separated the light from the darkness. "Let there be light!" he said. God created twinkling stars and a glowing moon. He made puffy clouds and a shining sun too.

Use the stickers to fill the sky with stars and a moon.

Do you know how to draw a star? Trace the star below.

Draw a sun. Add rays. Color the sun.

Connect the dots to finish the picture. Then color it in.

A Beautiful World

God also made plants of many shapes and colors. He made mountains, hills, and valleys.

All Creatures Big and Small

On the fifth day of creation, God made swishy fish and squiggly creatures to live in the ocean. He made birds to fly across the sky.

Use the stickers to fill the ocean with fish and the sky with birds.

Do you know which sea creature sticker is the *octopus*? Hint: Look for eight limbs. Count them.

What's the Difference?

On the sixth day, God created animals to creep, crawl, hop, and gallop. Then from the dust, God made the most wonderful creature of all—a person. God named him Adam.

Find the differences between the two pictures. Circle them. Hint: There are five.

Trace ADAM'S name.

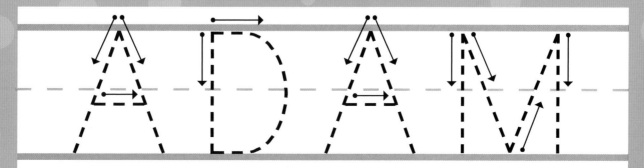

Color in the animals.

The Name Game

God asked Adam to name all the animals.
Can you name each animal as you color it in?

Draw a line to match the male and female animals.

The Animal Family

Where Is Eve?

Adam loved all the animals, but he could not find a friend that was just right for him. So God created a woman. Her name was Eve.

Help Adam find Eve.

In His Image

God said he created people "in his image." This means God wants us to try to be like him. God was an artist. He created a beautiful world. You can be an artist too. Draw a picture of yourself and your family. Don't forget your pets!

The Garden Search

Together, Adam and Eve took care of God's garden. God told them they could eat from any tree in the garden except for one. They must never eat the fruit from the tree of the knowledge of good and evil.

Use the stickers to fill the tree with fruit.

Find and circle the words in the puzzle.

Fruit
Garden
Leaf
Tree
Trunk
Adam
Eve

N	R	T	R	E	E	Q
Y	E	G	G	M	I	T
W	F	A	E	L	Z	R
I	R	R	V	E	A	U
L	U	D	E	A	D	N
P	I	E	U	F	A	K
D	T	N	F	W	M	N

Animals All Around

Use the stickers to add animals to the garden.
Add Adam and Eve too.

Can you find the snake? Circle it.

Count It Out

How many of each? Circle the number.

| | | | 1 | 2 | (3) |

| | | | 2 | 3 | 4 |

| | | 1 | 2 | 3 |

| | | 4 | 5 | 6 |

| | | 4 | 5 | 6 |

The Sneaky Snake

There was a sneaky snake in the garden. One day, the snake saw Eve near the special tree. It hissed, "Did God *really* tell you not to eat fruit from this tree?" The snake wanted Eve to disobey God. "You should try some of this tasty fruit," it said.

What did Eve do? Solve the secret message.

E _ _ _   A _ _ _

_ _ _

_ _ _ _ _ .

The Forbidden Fruit

After Eve ate the fruit, she gave some to Adam. He took a bite too. As the sun was going down, Adam and Eve heard God walking through the garden. He was looking for them. Adam and Eve hid among the trees because they were afraid.

Look at the pictures. Write the numbers 1, 2, 3, 4 to show the order things happened.

15

Color in the picture.

Knowledge of Good and Evil

God told Adam and Eve they had to leave the garden because of what they had done. He placed angels and a flaming sword at the entrance. Adam and Eve would not be allowed in the garden again. But God would always love them.